TOY SHOP
AND TWO OTHERS

CW01095848

TOY SHOP
AND TWO OTHERS

HARRY HARRISON

WILDSIDE PRESS

TOY SHOP

"Top Shop" was originally published in *Analog*, April 1962. "The Repairman" was originally published in *Galaxy* ,February 1958. "The K-Factor" was originally published in *Analog*, December 1960.

This edition published in 2009 by Wildside Press, LLC.
www.wildsidepress.com

CONTENTS

TOY SHOP

Because there were few adults in the crowd, and Colonel "Biff" Hawton stood over six feet tall, he could see every detail of the demonstration. The children — and most of the parents — gaped in wide-eyed wonder. Biff Hawton was too sophisticated to be awed. He stayed on because he wanted to find out what the trick was that made the gadget work.

"It's all explained right here in your instruction book," the demonstrator said, holding up a garishly printed booklet opened to a four-color diagram. "You all know how magnets pick up things and I bet you even know that the earth itself is one great big magnet — that's why compasses always point north. Well . . . the Atomic Wonder Space Wave Tapper hangs onto those space waves. Invisibly all about us, and even going right through us, are the magnetic waves of the earth. The Atomic Wonder rides these waves just the way a ship rides the waves in the ocean. Now watch. . . ."

Every eye was on him as he put the gaudy model rocketship on top of the table and stepped back. It was made of stamped metal and seemed as incapable of flying as a can of ham — which it very much resembled. Neither wings, propellors, nor jets broke through the painted surface. It rested on three rubber wheels and coming out through the bottom was a double strand of thin insulated wire. This white wire ran across the top of the black table and terminated in a control box in the demonstrator's hand. An indicator light, a switch and a knob appeared to be the only controls.

"I turn on the Power Switch, sending a surge of current to the Wave Receptors," he said. The switch clicked and the light blinked on and off with a steady pulse. Then the man began to slowly turn the knob. "A careful touch on the Wave Generator is necessary as we are dealing with the powers of the whole world here. . . ."

A concerted *ahhhh* swept through the crowd as the Space Wave Tapper shivered a bit, then rose slowly into the air. The demonstrator stepped back and the toy rose higher and higher, bobbing gently on the invisible waves of magnetic force that supported it. Ever so slowly the power was reduced and it settled back to the table.

"Only $17.95," the young man said, putting a large price sign on the table. "For the complete set of the Atomic Wonder, the Space Tapper control box, battery and instruction book . . ."

At the appearance of the price card the crowd broke up noisily and the children rushed away towards the operating model trains. The demonstrator's words were lost in their noisy passage, and after a moment he sank into a gloomy silence. He put the control box down, yawned and sat on the edge of the table. Colonel Hawton was the only one left after the crowd had moved on.

"Could you tell me how this thing works?" the colonel asked, coming forward. The demonstrator brightened up and picked up one of the toys.

"Well, if you will look here, sir. . . ." He opened the hinged top. "You will see the Space Wave coils at each end of the ship." With a pencil he pointed out the odd shaped plastic forms about an inch in diameter that had been wound — apparently at random — with a few turns of copper wire. Except for these coils the interior of the model was empty. The coils were wired together and other wires ran out through the hole in the bottom of the control box. Biff Hawton turned a very quizzical eye on the gadget and upon the demonstrator who completely ignored this sign of disbelief.

"Inside the control box is the battery," the young man said, snapping it open and pointing to an ordinary flashlight battery. "The current goes through the Power Switch and Power Light to the Wave Generator . . ."

"What you mean to say," Biff broke in, "is that the juice from this fifteen cent battery goes through this cheap rheostat to those meaningless coils in the model and absolutely nothing happens. Now tell me what really flies the thing. If I'm going to drop eighteen bucks for six-bits worth of tin, I want to know what I'm getting."

The demonstrator flushed. "I'm sorry, sir," he stammered. "I wasn't trying to hide anything. Like any magic trick this one can't be really demonstrated until it has been purchased." He leaned forward and whispered confidentially. "I'll tell you what I'll do though. This thing is way overpriced and hasn't been moving at all. The manager said I could let them go at three dollars if I could find any takers. If you want to buy it for that price. . . ."

"Sold, my boy!" the colonel said, slamming three bills down

on the table. "I'll give that much for it no matter *how* it works. The boys in the shop will get a kick out of it," he tapped the winged rocket on his chest. "Now *really* — what holds it up?"

The demonstrator looked around carefully, then pointed. "Strings!" he said. "Or rather a black thread. It runs from the top of the model, through a tiny loop in the ceiling, and back down to my hand — tied to this ring on my finger. When I back up — the model rises. It's as simple as that."

"All good illusions are simple," the colonel grunted, tracing the black thread with his eye. "As long as there is plenty of flim-flam to distract the viewer."

"If you don't have a black table, a black cloth will do," the young man said. "And the arch of a doorway is a good site, just see that the room in back is dark."

"Wrap it up, my boy, I wasn't born yesterday. I'm an old hand at this kind of thing."

Biff Hawton sprang it at the next Thursday-night poker party. The gang were all missile men and they cheered and jeered as he hammered up the introduction.

"Let me copy the diagram, Biff, I could use some of those magnetic waves in the new bird!"

"Those flashlight batteries are cheaper than lox, this is the thing of the future!"

Only Teddy Kaner caught wise as the flight began. He was an amateur magician and spotted the gimmick at once. He kept silent with professional courtesy, and smiled ironically as the rest of the bunch grew silent one by one. The colonel was a good showman and he had set the scene well. He almost had them believing in the Space Wave Tapper before he was through. When the model had landed and he had switched it off he couldn't stop them from crowding around the table.

"A thread!" one of the engineers shouted, almost with relief, and they all laughed along with him.

"Too bad," the head project physicist said, "I was hoping that a little Space Wave Tapping could help us out. Let me try a flight with it."

"Teddy Kaner first," Biff announced. "He spotted it while you were all watching the flashing lights, only he didn't say anything."

Kaner slipped the ring with the black thread over his finger and started to step back.

"You have to turn the switch on first," Biff said.

"I know," Kaner smiled. "But that's part of illusion — the spiel and the misdirection. I'm going to try this cold first, so I can get it moving up and down smoothly, then go through it with the whole works."

He moved his hand back smoothly, in a professional manner that drew no attention to it. The model lifted from the table — then crashed back down.

"The thread broke," Kaner said.

"You jerked it, instead of pulling smoothly," Biff said and knotted the broken thread. "Here let me show you how to do it."

The thread broke again when Biff tried it, which got a good laugh that made his collar a little warm. Someone mentioned the poker game.

This was the only time that poker was mentioned or even remembered that night. Because very soon after this they found that the thread would lift the model only when the switch was on and two and a half volts flowing through the joke coils. With the current turned off the model was too heavy to lift. The thread broke every time.

"I still think it's a screwy idea," the young man said. "One week getting fallen arches, demonstrating those toy ships for every brat within a thousand miles. Then selling the things for three bucks when they must have cost at least a hundred dollars apiece to make."

"But you *did* sell the ten of them to people who would be interested?" the older man asked.

"I think so, I caught a few Air Force officers and a colonel in missiles one day. Then there was one official I remembered from the Bureau of Standards. Luckily he didn't recognize me. Then those two professors you spotted from the university."

"Then the problem is out of our hands and into theirs. All we have to do now is sit back and wait for results."

"*What* results?! These people weren't interested when we were hammering on their doors with the proof. We've patented the coils and can prove to anyone that there is a reduction in weight around them when they are operating. . . ."

"But a small reduction. And we don't know what is causing it. No one can be interested in a thing like that — a fractional weight decrease in a clumsy model, certainly not enough to lift the weight of the generator. No one wrapped up in massive fuel consumption, tons of lift and such is going to have time to worry about a crackpot who thinks he has found a minor slip in Newton's laws."

"You think they will now?" the young man asked, cracking his knuckles impatiently.

"I *know* they will. The tensile strength of that thread is correctly adjusted to the weight of the model. The thread will break if you try to lift the model with it. Yet you can lift the model — after a small increment of its weight has been removed by the coils. This is going to bug these men. Nobody is going to ask them to solve the problem or concern themselves with it. But it will nag at them because they know this effect can't possibly exist. They'll see at once that the magnetic-wave theory is nonsense. Or perhaps true? We don't know. But they will all be thinking about it and worrying about it. Someone is going to experiment in his basement — just as a hobby of course — to find the cause of the error. And he or someone else is going to find out what makes those coils work, or maybe a way to improve them!"

"And we have the patents. . . ."

"Correct. They will be doing the research that will take them out of the massive-lift-propulsion business and into the field of pure space flight."

"And in doing so they will be making us rich — whenever the time comes to manufacture," the young man said cynically.

"We'll all be rich, son," the older man said, patting him on the shoulder. "Believe me, you're not going to recognize this old world ten years from now."

THE REPAIRMAN

The Old Man had that look of intense glee on his face that meant someone was in for a very rough time. Since we were alone, it took no great feat of intelligence to figure it would be me. I talked first, bold attack being the best defense and so forth.

"I quit. Don't bother telling me what dirty job you have cooked up, because I have already quit and you do not want to reveal company secrets to me."

The grin was even wider now and he actually chortled as he thumbed a button on his console. A thick legal document slid out of the delivery slot onto his desk.

"This is your contract," he said. "It tells how and when you will work. A steel-and-vanadium-bound contract that you couldn't crack with a molecular disruptor."

I leaned out quickly, grabbed it and threw it into the air with a single motion. Before it could fall, I had my Solar out and, with a wide-angle shot, burned the contract to ashes.

The Old Man pressed the button again and another contract slid out on his desk. If possible, the smile was still wider now.

"I should have said a *duplicate* of your contract — like this one here." He made a quick note on his secretary plate. "I have deducted 13 credits from your salary for the cost of the duplicate — as well as a 100-credit fine for firing a Solar inside a building."

I slumped, defeated, waiting for the blow to land. The Old Man fondled my contract.

"According to this document, you can't quit. Ever. Therefore I have a little job I know you'll enjoy. Repair job. The Centauri beacon has shut down. It's a Mark III beacon...."

"*What* kind of beacon?" I asked him. I have repaired hyper-space beacons from one arm of the Galaxy to the other and was sure I had worked on every type or model made. But I had never heard of this kind.

"Mark III," the Old Man repeated, practically chortling. "I never heard of it either until Records dug up the specs. They found them buried in the back of their oldest warehouse. This was the earliest type of beacon ever built — by Earth, no less. Considering its location on one of the Proxima Centauri planets, it might very well be the first beacon."

I looked at the blueprints he handed me and felt my eyes glaze with horror. "It's a monstrosity! It looks more like a distillery than a beacon — must be at least a few hundred meters high. I'm a repairman, not an archeologist. This pile of junk is over 2000 years old. Just forget about it and build a new one."

The Old Man leaned over his desk, breathing into my face. "It would take a year to install a new beacon — besides being too expensive — and this relic is on one of the main routes. We have ships making fifteen-light-year detours now."

He leaned back, wiped his hands on his handkerchief and gave me Lecture Forty-four on Company Duty and My Troubles.

"This department is officially called Maintenance and Repair, when it really should be called trouble-shooting. Hyperspace beacons are made to last forever — or damn close to it. When one of them breaks down, it is *never* an accident, and repairing the thing is never a matter of just plugging in a new part."

He was telling *me* — the guy who did the job while he sat back on his fat paycheck in an air-conditioned office.

He rambled on. "How I wish that were all it took! I would have a fleet of parts ships and junior mechanics to install them. But its not like that at all. I have a fleet of expensive ships that are equipped to do almost anything — manned by a bunch of irresponsibles like *you*."

I nodded moodily at his pointing finger.

"How I wish I could fire you all! Combination space-jockeys, mechanics, engineers, soldiers, con-men and anything else it takes to do the repairs. I have to browbeat, bribe, blackmail and bulldoze you thugs into doing a simple job. If you think you're fed up, just think how I feel. But the ships must go through! The beacons must operate!"

I recognized this deathless line as the curtain speech and crawled to my feet. He threw the Mark III file at me and went back to scratching in his papers. Just as I reached the door, he looked up and impaled me on his finger again.

"And don't get any fancy ideas about jumping your contract. We can attach that bank account of yours on Algol II long before you could draw the money out."

I smiled, a little weakly, I'm afraid, as if I had never meant to keep that account a secret. His spies were getting more efficient every day. Walking down the hall, I tried to figure a way to transfer the money without his catching on — and knew at the same time he was figuring a way to outfigure me.

It was all very depressing, so I stopped for a drink, then went on to the spaceport.

By the time the ship was serviced, I had a course charted. The nearest beacon to the broken-down Proxima Centauri Beacon was on one of the planets of Beta Circinus and I headed there first, a short trip of only about nine days in hyperspace.

To understand the importance of the beacons, you have to understand hyperspace. Not that many people do, but it is easy enough to understand that in this *non*-space the regular rules don't apply. Speed and measurements are a matter of relationship, not constant facts like the fixed universe.

The first ships to enter hyperspace had no place to go — and no way to even tell if they had moved. The beacons solved that problem and opened the entire universe. They are built on planets and generate tremendous amounts of power. This power is turned into radiation that is punched through into hyperspace. Every beacon has a code signal as part of its radiation and represents a measurable point in hyperspace. Triangulation and quadrature of the beacons works for navigation — only it follows its own rules. The rules are complex and variable, but they are still rules that a navigator can follow.

For a hyperspace jump, you need at least four beacons for an accurate fix. For long jumps, navigators use as many as seven or eight. So every beacon is important and every one has to keep operating. That is where I and the other trouble-shooters came in.

We travel in well-stocked ships that carry a little bit of everything; only one man to a ship because that is all it takes to operate the overly efficient repair machinery. Due to the very nature of our job, we spend most of our time just rocketing through normal space. After all, when a beacon breaks down, how do you find it?

Not through hyperspace. All you can do is approach as close as you can by using other beacons, then finish the trip in normal space. This can take months, and often does.

This job didn't turn out to be quite that bad. I zeroed on the Beta Circinus beacon and ran a complicated eight-point problem through the navigator, using every beacon I could get an accurate fix on. The computer gave me a course with an estimated point-of-arrival as well as a built-in safety factor I never could eliminate from the machine.

I would much rather take a chance of breaking through near some star than spend time just barreling through normal space, but apparently Tech knows this, too. They had a safety factor built into the computer so you couldn't end up inside a star no matter how hard you tried. I'm sure there was no humaneness in this decision. They just didn't want to lose the ship.

It was a twenty-hour jump, ship's time, and I came through in the middle of nowhere. The robot analyzer chuckled to itself and scanned all the stars, comparing them to the spectra of Proxima Centauri. It finally rang a bell and blinked a light. I peeped through the eyepiece.

A fast reading with the photocell gave me the apparent magnitude and a comparison with its absolute magnitude showed its distance. Not as bad as I had thought — a six-week run, give or take a few days. After feeding a course tape into the robot pilot, I strapped into the acceleration tank and went to sleep.

The time went fast. I rebuilt my camera for about the twentieth time and just about finished a correspondence course in nucleonics. Most repairmen take these courses. Besides their always coming in handy, the company grades your pay by the number of specialties you can handle. All this, with some oil painting and free-fall workouts in the gym, passed the time. I was asleep when the alarm went off that announced planetary distance.

Planet two, where the beacon was situated according to the old charts, was a mushy-looking, wet kind of globe. I tried to make sense out of the ancient directions and finally located the right area. Staying outside the atmosphere, I sent a flying eye down to look things over. In this business, you learn early when and where to risk your own skin. The eye would be good enough for the preliminary survey.

The old boys had enough brains to choose a traceable site for the beacon, equidistant on a line between two of the most prominent mountain peaks. I located the peaks easily enough and started the eye out from the first peak and kept it on a course directly toward the second. There was a nose and tail radar in the eye and I fed their signals into a scope as an amplitude curve. When the two peaks coincided, I spun the eye controls and dived the thing down.

I cut out the radar and cut in the nose orthicon and sat back to watch the beacon appear on the screen.

The image blinked, focused — and a great damn pyramid swam into view. I cursed and wheeled the eye in circles, scanning the surrounding country. It was flat, marshy bottom land without a bump. The only thing in a ten-mile circle was this pyramid — and that definitely wasn't my beacon.

Or wasn't it?

I dived the eye lower. The pyramid was a crude-looking thing of undressed stone, without carvings or decorations. There was a shimmer of light from the top and I took a closer look at it. On the peak of the pyramid was a hollow basin filled with water. When I saw that, something clicked in my mind.

Locking the eye in a circular course, I dug through the Mark III plans — and there it was. The beacon had a precipitating field and a basin on top of it for water; this was used to cool the reactor that powered the monstrosity. If the water was still there, the beacon was still there — inside the pyramid. The natives, who, of course, weren't even mentioned by the idiots who constructed the thing, had built a nice heavy, thick stone pyramid around the beacon.

I took another look at the screen and realized that I had locked the eye into a circular orbit about twenty feet above the pyramid. The summit of the stone pile was now covered with lizards of some type, apparently the local life-form. They had what looked like throwing sticks and arbalasts and were trying to shoot down the eye, a cloud of arrows and rocks flying in every direction.

I pulled the eye straight up and away and threw in the control circuit that would return it automatically to the ship.

Then I went to the galley for a long, strong drink. My beacon was not only locked inside a mountain of handmade stone, but I had managed to irritate the things who had built the pyramid. A great beginning for a job and one clearly designed to drive a stronger man than me to the bottle.

Normally, a repairman stays away from native cultures. They are poison. Anthropologists may not mind being dissected for their science, but a repairman wants to make no sacrifices of any kind for his job. For this reason, most beacons are built on uninhabited planets. If a beacon *has* to go on a planet with a culture, it is usually built in some inaccessible place.

Why this beacon had been built within reach of the local claws, I had yet to find out. But that would come in time. The first thing to do was make contact. To make contact, you have to know the local language.

And, for *that*, I had long before worked out a system that was fool-proof.

I had a pryeye of my own construction. It looked like a piece of rock about a foot long. Once on the ground, it would never be noticed, though it was a little disconcerting to see it float by. I located a lizard town about a thousand kilometers from the pyramid and dropped the eye. It swished down and landed at night in the bank of the local mud wallow. This was a favorite spot that drew a good crowd during the day. In the morning, when the first wallowers arrived, I flipped on the recorder.

After about five of the local days, I had a sea of native conversation in the memory bank of the machine translator and had tagged a few expressions. This is fairly easy to do when you have a machine memory to work with. One of the lizards gargled at another one and the second one turned around. I tagged this expression with the phrase, "Hey, George!" and waited my chance to use it. Later the same day, I caught one of them alone and shouted "Hey, George!" at him. It gurgled out through the speaker in the local tongue and he turned around.

When you get enough reference phrases like this in the memory bank, the MT brain takes over and starts filling in the missing pieces. As soon as the MT could give a running translation of any conversation it heard, I figured it was time to make a contact.

I found him easily enough. He was the Centaurian version of a goat-boy — he herded a particularly loathsome form of local life in the swamps outside the town. I had one of the working eyes dig a cave in an outcropping of rock and wait for him.

When he passed next day, I whispered into the mike: "Welcome, O Goat-boy Grandson! This is your grandfather's spirit speaking from paradise." This fitted in with what I could make out of the local religion.

Goat-boy stopped as if he'd been shot. Before he could move, I pushed a switch and a handful of the local currency, wampum-type shells, rolled out of the cave and landed at his feet.

"Here is some money from paradise, because you have been a good boy." Not really from paradise — I had lifted it from the treasury the night before. "Come back tomorrow and we will talk some more," I called after the fleeing figure. I was pleased to notice that he took the cash before taking off.

After that, Grandpa in paradise had many heart-to-heart talks with Grandson, who found the heavenly loot more than he could resist. Grandpa had been out of touch with things since his death and Goat-boy happily filled him in.

I learned all I needed to know of the history, past and recent, and it wasn't nice.

In addition to the pyramid being around the beacon, there was a nice little religious war going on around the pyramid.

It all began with the land bridge. Apparently the local lizards had been living in the swamps when the beacon was built, but the builders didn't think much of them. They were a low type and confined to a distant continent. The idea that the race would develop and might reach *this* continent never occurred to the beacon mechanics. Which is, of course, what happened.

A little geological turnover, a swampy land bridge formed in the right spot, and the lizards began to wander up beacon valley. And found religion. A shiny metal temple out of which poured a constant stream of magic water — the reactor-cooling water pumped down from the atmosphere condenser on the roof. The radioactivity in the water didn't hurt the natives. It caused mutations that bred true.

A city was built around the temple and, through the centuries, the pyramid was put up around the beacon. A special branch of the priesthood served the temple. All went well until one of the priests violated the temple and destroyed the holy waters. There had been revolt, strife, murder and destruction since then. But still the holy waters would not flow. Now armed mobs fought around the temple each day and a new band of priests guarded the sacred fount.

And I had to walk into the middle of that mess and repair the thing.

It would have been easy enough if we were allowed a little mayhem. I could have had a lizard fry, fixed the beacon and taken off. Only "native life-forms" were quite well protected. There were spy cells on my ship, all of which I hadn't found, that would cheerfully rat on me when I got back.

Diplomacy was called for. I sighed and dragged out the plasti-flesh equipment.

Working from 3D snaps of Grandson, I modeled a passable reptile head over my own features. It was a little short in the jaw, me not having one of their toothy mandibles, but that was all right. I didn't have to look *exactly* like them, just something close, to soothe the native mind. It's logical. If I were an ignorant aborigine of Earth and I ran into a Spican, who looks like a two-foot gob of dried shellac, I would immediately leave the scene. However, if the Spican was wearing a suit of plastiflesh that looked remotely humanoid, I would at least stay and talk to him. This was what I was aiming to do with the Centaurians.

When the head was done, I peeled it off and attached it to an attractive suit of green plastic, complete with tail. I was really glad they had tails. The lizards didn't wear clothes and I wanted to take along a lot of electronic equipment. I built the tail over a metal frame that anchored around my waist. Then I filled the frame with all the equipment I would need and began to wire the suit.

When it was done, I tried it on in front of a full-length mirror. It was horrible but effective. The tail dragged me down in the rear and gave me a duck-waddle, but that only helped the resemblance.

That night I took the ship down into the hills nearest the pyramid, an out-of-the-way dry spot where the amphibious natives would never go. A little before dawn, the eye hooked onto my shoulders and we sailed straight up. We hovered above the temple at about 2,000 meters, until it was light, then dropped straight down.

It must have been a grand sight. The eye was camouflaged to look like a flying lizard, sort of a cardboard pterodactyl, and the slowly flapping wings obviously had nothing to do with our flight. But it was impressive enough for the natives. The first one that spotted me screamed and dropped over on his back. The others came running. They milled and mobbed and piled on top of one another, and by that time I had landed in the plaza fronting the temple. The priesthood arrived.

I folded my arms in a regal stance. "Greetings, O noble servers of the Great God," I said. Of course I didn't say it out loud, just whispered loud enough for the throat mike to catch. This was radioed back to the MT and the translation shot back to a speaker in my jaws.

The natives chomped and rattled and the translation rolled out almost instantly. I had the volume turned up and the whole square echoed.

Some of the more credulous natives prostrated themselves and others fled screaming. One doubtful type raised a spear, but no one else tried that after the pterodactyl-eye picked him up and dropped him in the swamp. The priests were a hard-headed lot and weren't buying any lizards in a poke; they just stood and muttered. I had to take the offensive again.

"Begone, O faithful steed," I said to the eye, and pressed the control in my palm at the same time.

It took off straight up a bit faster than I wanted; little pieces of wind-torn plastic rained down. While the crowd was ogling this ascent, I walked through the temple doors.

"I would talk with you, O noble priests," I said.

Before they could think up a good answer, I was inside.

The temple was a small one built against the base of the pyramid. I hoped I wasn't breaking too many taboos by going in. I wasn't stopped, so it looked all right. The temple was a single room with a murky-looking pool at one end. Sloshing in the pool was an ancient reptile who clearly was one of the leaders. I waddled toward him and he gave me a cold and fishy eye, then growled something.

The MT whispered into my ear, "Just what in the name of the thirteenth sin are you and what are you doing here?"

I drew up my scaly figure in a noble gesture and pointed toward the ceiling. "I come from your ancestors to help you. I am here to restore the Holy Waters."

This raised a buzz of conversation behind me, but got no rise out of the chief. He sank slowly into the water until only his eyes were showing. I could almost hear the wheels turning behind that moss-covered forehead. Then he lunged up and pointed a dripping finger at me.

"You are a liar! You are no ancestor of ours! We will —"

"Stop!" I thundered before he got so far in that he couldn't back out. "I said your ancestors sent me as emissary — I am not one of your ancestors. Do not try to harm me or the wrath of those who have Passed On will turn against you."

When I said this, I turned to jab a claw at the other priests, using the motion to cover my flicking a coin grenade toward them. It blew a nice hole in the floor with a great show of noise and smoke.

The First Lizard knew I was talking sense then and immediately called a meeting of the shamans. It, of course, took place in the public bathtub and I had to join them there. We jawed and gurgled for about an hour and settled all the major points.

I found out that they were new priests; the previous ones had all been boiled for letting the Holy Waters cease. They found out I was there only to help them restore the flow of the waters. They bought this, tentatively, and we all heaved out of the tub and trickled muddy paths across the floor. There was a bolted and guarded door that led into the pyramid proper. While it was being opened, the First Lizard turned to me.

"Undoubtedly you know of the rule," he said. "Because the old priests did pry and peer, it was ruled henceforth that only the blind could enter the Holy of Holies." I'd swear he was smiling, if thirty teeth peeking out of what looked like a crack in an old suit-case can be called smiling.

He was also signaling to him an underpriest who carried a bra-zier of charcoal complete with red-hot irons. All I could do was stand and watch as he stirred up the coals, pulled out the ruddiest iron and turned toward me. He was just drawing a bead on my right eyeball when my brain got back in gear.

"Of course," I said, "blinding is only right. But in my case you will have to blind me before I *leave* the Holy of Holies, not now. I need my eyes to see and mend the Fount of Holy Waters. Once the waters flow again, I will laugh as I hurl myself on the burning iron."

He took a good thirty seconds to think it over and had to agree with me. The local torturer sniffled a bit and threw a little more charcoal on the fire. The gate crashed open and I stalked through; then it banged to behind me and I was alone in the dark.

But not for long — there was a shuffling nearby and I took a chance and turned on my flash. Three priests were groping toward me, their eye-sockets red pits of burned flesh. They knew what I wanted and led the way without a word.

A crumbling and cracked stone stairway brought us up to a solid metal doorway labeled in archaic script *MARK III BEACON — AUTHORIZED PERSONNEL ONLY.* The trusting builders counted on the sign to do the whole job, for there wasn't a trace of a lock on the door. One lizard merely turned the handle and we were inside the beacon.

I unzipped the front of my camouflage suit and pulled out the blueprints. With the faithful priests stumbling after me, I located the control room and turned on the lights. There was a residue of charge in the emergency batteries, just enough to give a dim light. The meters and indicators looked to be in good shape; if anything, unexpectedly bright from constant polishing.

I checked the readings carefully and found just what I had sus-pected. One of the eager lizards had managed to open a circuit box and had polished the switches inside. While doing this, he had thrown one of the switches and that had caused the trouble.

*   *   *

Rather, that had *started* the trouble. It wasn't going to be ended by just reversing the water-valve switch. This valve was supposed to be used only for repairs, after the pile was damped. When the water was cut off with the pile in operation, it had started to over-heat and the automatic safeties had dumped the charge down the pit.

I could start the water again easily enough, but there was no fuel left in the reactor.

I wasn't going to play with the fuel problem at all. It would be far easier to install a new power plant. I had one in the ship that was about a tenth the size of the ancient bucket of bolts and produced at least four times the power. Before I sent for it, I checked over the rest of the beacon. In 2000 years, there should be *some* sign of wear.

The old boys had built well, I'll give them credit for that. Ninety per cent of the machinery had no moving parts and had suffered no wear whatever. Other parts they had beefed up, figuring they would wear, but slowly. The water-feed pipe from the roof, for example. The pipe walls were at least three meters thick — and the pipe opening itself no bigger than my head. There were some things I could do, though, and I made a list of parts.

The parts, the new power plant and a few other odds and ends were chuted into a neat pile on the ship. I checked all the parts by screen before they were loaded in a metal crate. In the darkest hour before dawn, the heavy-duty eye dropped the crate outside the temple and darted away without being seen.

I watched the priests through the pryeye while they tried to open it. When they had given up, I boomed orders at them through a speaker in the crate. They spent most of the day sweating the heavy box up through the narrow temple stairs and I enjoyed a good sleep. It was resting inside the beacon door when I woke up.

The repairs didn't take long, though there was plenty of groaning from the blind lizards when they heard me ripping the wall open to get at the power leads. I even hooked a gadget to the water pipe so their Holy Waters would have the usual refreshing radioactivity when they started flowing again. The moment this was all finished, I did the job they were waiting for.

I threw the switch that started the water flowing again.

There were a few minutes while the water began to gurgle down through the dry pipe. Then a roar came from outside the pyramid that must have shaken its stone walls. Shaking my hands once over my head, I went down for the eye-burning ceremony.

The blind lizards were waiting for me by the door and looked even unhappier than usual. When I tried the door, I found out why — it was bolted and barred from the other side.

"It has been decided," a lizard said, "that you shall remain here forever and tend the Holy Waters. We will stay with you and serve your every need."

A delightful prospect, eternity spent in a locked beacon with three blind lizards. In spite of their hospitality, I couldn't accept.

"What — you dare interfere with the messenger of your ancestors!" I had the speaker on full volume and the vibration almost shook my head off.

The lizards cringed and I set my Solar for a narrow beam and ran it around the door jamb. There was a great crunching and banging from the junk piled against it, and then the door swung free. I threw it open. Before they could protest, I had pushed the priests out through it.

The rest of their clan showed up at the foot of the stairs and made a great ruckus while I finished welding the door shut. Running through the crowd, I faced up to the First Lizard in his tub. He sank slowly beneath the surface.

"What lack of courtesy!" I shouted. He made little bubbles in the water. "The ancestors are annoyed and have decided to forbid entrance to the Inner Temple forever; though, out of kindness, they will let the waters flow. Now I must return — on with the ceremony!"

The torture-master was too frightened to move, so I grabbed out his hot iron. A touch on the side of my face dropped a steel plate over my eyes, under the plastiskin. Then I jammed the iron hard into my phony eye-sockets and the plastic gave off an authentic odor.

A cry went up from the crowd as I dropped the iron and staggered in blind circles. I must admit it went off pretty well.

Before they could get any more bright ideas, I threw the switch and my plastic pterodactyl sailed in through the door. I couldn't see it, of course, but I knew it had arrived when the grapples in the claws latched onto the steel plates on my shoulders.

I had got turned around after the eye-burning and my flying beast hooked onto me backward. I had meant to sail out bravely, blind eyes facing into the sunset; instead, I faced the crowd as I soared away, so I made the most of a bad situation and threw them a snappy military salute. Then I was out in the fresh air and away.

When I lifted the plate and poked holes in the seared plastic, I could see the pyramid growing smaller behind me, water gushing out of the base and a happy crowd of reptiles sporting in its radio-active rush. I counted off on my talons to see if I had forgotten anything.

One: The beacon was repaired.

Two: The door was sealed, so there should be no more sabotage, accidental or deliberate.

Three: The priests should be satisfied. The water was running again, my eyes had been duly burned out, and they were back in business. Which added up to —

Four: The fact that they would probably let another repairman in, under the same conditions, if the beacon conked out again. At least I had done nothing, like butchering a few of them, that would make them antagonistic toward future ancestral messengers.

I stripped off my tattered lizard suit back in the ship, very glad that it would be some other repairman who'd get the job.

THE K-FACTOR

"We're losing a planet, Neel. I'm afraid that I can't . . . understand it."

The bald and wrinkled head wobbled a bit on the thin neck, and his eyes were moist. Abravanel was a very old man. Looking at him, Neel realized for the first time just how old and close to death he was. It was a profoundly shocking thought.

"Pardon me, sir," Neel broke in, "but is it possible? To lose a planet, I mean. If the readings are done correctly, and the k-factor equations worked to the tenth decimal place, then it's really just a matter of adjustment, making the indicated corrections. After all, Societics is an exact science —"

"Exact? *Exact!* Of course it's not! Have I taught you so little that you dare say that to me?" Anger animated the old man, driving the shadow of death back a step or two.

Neel hesitated, feeling his hands quiver ever so slightly, groping for the right words. Societics was his faith, and his teacher, Abravanel, its only prophet. This man before him, carefully preserved by the age-retarding drugs, was unique in the galaxy. A living anachronism, a refugee from the history books. Abravanel had singlehandedly worked out the equations, spelled out his science of Societics. Then he had trained seven generations of students in its fundamentals. Hearing the article of his faith defamed by its creator produced a negative feedback loop in Neel so strong his hands vibrated in tune with it. It took a jarring effort to crack out of the cycle.

"The laws that control Societics, as postulated by . . . you, are as exact as any others in the unified-field theory universe."

"No they're not. And, if any man I taught believes that nonsense, I'm retiring tomorrow and dropping dead the day after. My science — and it is really not logical to call it a science — is based on observation, experimentation, control groups and corrected observations. And though we have made observations in the millions, we are dealing in units in the billions, and the interactions of these units are multiples of that. And let us never forget that our units are people who, when they operate as individuals, do so in a completely different manner. So you cannot truthfully call my theories exact. They fit the facts well enough and produce results in practice, that has been empirically proven. So far. Some day, I am sure, we will run across a culture that doesn't fit my rules. At that time the rules will have to be revised. We may have that situation now on Himmel. There's trouble cooking there."

"They have always had a high activity count, sir," Neel put in hopefully.

"High yes, but *always* negative. Until now. Now it is slightly positive and nothing we can do seems to change it. That's why I've called you in. I want you to run a new basic survey, ignoring the old one still in operation, to re-examine the check points on our graphs. The trouble may lie there."

Neel thought before he answered, picking his words carefully. "Wouldn't that be a little . . . unethical, sir? After all Hengly, who is operator there now, is a friend of mine. Going behind his back, you know."

"I know nothing of the sort." Abravanel snorted. "We are not playing for poker chips, or seeing who can get a paper published first. Have you forgotten what Societics is?"

Neel answered by rote. "The applied study of the interaction of individuals in a culture, the interaction of the group generated by these individuals, the equations derived therefrom, and the application of these equations to control one or more factors of this same culture."

"And what is the one factor that we have tried to control in order to make all the other factors possible of existence?"

"War." Neel said, in a very small voice.

"Very good then, there is no doubt what it is we are talking about. You are going to land quietly on Himmel, do a survey as quickly as possible and transmit the data back here. There is no cause to think of it as sneaking behind Hengly's back, but as doing something to help him set the matter right. Is that understood?"

"Yes, sir," Neel said firmly this time, straightening his back and letting his right hand rest reassuringly on the computer slung from his belt.

"Excellent. Then it is now time to meet your assistant." Abravanel touched a button on his desk.

It was an unexpected development and Neel waited with

interest as the door opened. But he turned away abruptly, his eyes slitted and his face white with anger. Abravanel introduced them.

"Neel Sidorak, this is —"

"Costa. I know him. He was in my class for six months." There wasn't the slightest touch of friendliness in Neel's voice now. Abravanel either ignored it or didn't hear it. He went on as if the two cold, distant young men were the best of friends.

"Classmates. Very good — then there is no need to make introductions. Though it might be best to make clear your separate areas of control. This is your project Neel, and Adao Costa will be your assistant, following your orders and doing whatever he can to help. You know he isn't a graduate Societist, but he has done a lot of field work for us and can help you greatly in that. And, of course, he will be acting as an observer for the UN, and making his own reports in this connection."

Neel's anger was hot and apparent. "So he's a UN observer now. I wonder if he still holds his old job at the same time. I think it only fair, sir, that you know. He works for Interpol."

Abravanel's ancient and weary eyes looked at both men, and he sighed. "Wait outside Costa," he said, "Neel will be with you in a minute."

Costa left without a word and Abravanel waved Neel back to his chair. "Listen to me now," he said, "and stop playing tunes on that infernal buzzer." Neel snapped his hand away from the belt computer, as if it had suddenly grown hot. A hesitant finger reached out to clear the figures he had nervously been setting up, then thought better of it. Abravanel sucked life into his ancient pipe and squinted at the younger man.

"Listen," he said. "You have led a very sheltered life here at the university, and that is probably my fault. No, don't look angry, I don't mean about girls. In that matter undergraduates have been the same for centuries. I'm talking about people in groups, individuals, politics, and all the complicated mess that makes up human life. This has been your area of study and the program is carefully planned so you can study it secondhand. The important thing is to develop the abstract viewpoint, since any attempt to prejudge results can only mean disaster. And it has been proved many times that a man with a certain interest will make many unwitting errors to shape an observation or experiment in favor of his interest. No, we could have none of that here.

"We are following the proper study of mankind and we must do that by keeping personally on the outside, to preserve our perspective. When you understand that, you understand many small things about the university. Why we give only resident student scholarships at a young age, and why the out-of-the-way location here in the Dolomites. You will also see the reason why the campus bookstore stocks all of the books published, but never has an adequate supply of newspapers. The agreed policy has been to see that you all mature with the long view. Then — hopefully — you will be immune to short-term political interests after you leave.

"This policy has worked well in turning out men with the correct attitude towards their work. It has also turned out a fair number of self-centered, egocentric horrors."

Neel flushed. "Do you mean that I —"

"No, I don't mean you. If I did, I would say so. Your worst fault — if you can call it a fault, since it is the very thing we have been trying to bring about — is that you have a very provincial attitude towards the universe. Now is the time to re-examine some of those ideas. Firstly, what do you think the attitude of the UN is towards Societics?"

There was no easy answer, Neel could see traps ready for anything he said. His words were hesitant. "I can't say I've really ever thought about it. I imagine the UN would be in favor of it, since we make their job of world government that much easier —"

"No such thing," Abravanel said, tempering the sharpness of his words with a smile. "To put it in the simplest language, they hate our guts. They wish I had never formulated Societics, and at the same time they are very glad I did. They are in the position of the man who caught the tiger by the tail. The man enjoys watching the tiger eat all of his enemies, but as each one is consumed his worry grows greater. What will happen when the last one is gone? Will the tiger then turn and eat him?

"Well — we are the UN's tiger. Societics came along just at the time it was sorely needed. Earth had settled a number of planets, and governed them. First as outposts, then as colonies. The most advanced planets very quickly outgrew the colony stage and flexed their independent muscles. The UN had no particular desire to rule an empire, but at the same time they had to insure Earth's safety. I imagine they were considering all sorts of schemes — including outright military control — when they came to me.

"Even in its early, crude form, Societics provided a stopgap that would give them some breathing time. They saw to it that my work was well endowed and aided me — unofficially of course — in setting up the first control experiments on different planets. We had results, some very good, and the others not so bad that the local police couldn't get things back under control after a while. I was, of course, happy to perfect my theories in practice. After a hundred years I had all the rough spots evened down and we were in business. The UN has never come up with a workable alternative plan, so they have settled down to the uncomfortable business of holding the tiger's tail. They worry and spend vast sums of money keeping an eye on our work."

"But *why*?" Neel broke in.

"Why?" Abravanel gave a quick smile. "Thank you for fine character rating. I imagine it is inconceivable to you that I might want to be Emperor of the Universe. I could be, you know. The same forces that hold the lids on the planets could just as easily blow them off."

Neel was speechless at the awful enormity of the thought. Abravanel rose from behind his desk with an effort, and shambled over to lay a thin and feather-light arm on the younger man's shoulders. "Those are the facts of life my boy. And since we cannot escape them, we must live with them. Costa is just a man doing his duty. So try and put up with him. For my sake if not for your own."

"Of course," Neel agreed quickly. "The whole thing takes a bit of getting used to, but I think I can manage. We'll do as good a job on Himmel as it is possible to do. Don't worry about me, sir."

Costa was waiting in the next room, puffing quietly on a long cigarette. They left together, walking down the hall in silence. Neel glanced sideways at the wiry, dark-skinned Brazilian and wondered what he could say to smooth things out. He still had his reservations about Costa, but he'd keep them to himself now. Abravanel had ordered peace between them, and what the old man said was the law.

It was Costa who spoke first. "Can you brief me on Himmel — what we'll find there, and be expected to do?"

"Run the basic survey first, of course," Neel told him. "Chances are that that will be enough to straighten things out. Since the completion last year of the refining equations of Debir's Postulate, all sigma-110 and alpha-142 graph points are suspect —"

"Just stop there please, and run the flag back down the pole." Costa interrupted. "I had a six-months survey of Societics seven years ago, to give me a general idea of the field. I've worked with survey teams since then, but I have only the vaguest idea of the application of the information we got. Could you cover the ground again — only a bit slower?"

Neel controlled his anger successfully and started again, in his best classroom manner.

"Well, I'm sure you realize that a good survey is half the problem. It must be impartial and exact. If it is accurately done, application of the k-factor equations is almost mechanical."

"You've lost me again. Everyone always talks about the k-factor, but no one has ever explained just what it is."

Neel was warming to his topic now. "It's a term borrowed from nucleonics, and best understood in that context. Look, you know how an atomic pile works — essentially just like an atomic bomb. The difference is just a matter of degree and control. In both of them you have neutrons tearing around, some of them hitting nuclei and starting new neutrons going. These in turn hit and start others. This goes on faster and faster and *bam*, a few milliseconds later you have an atomic bomb. This is what happens if you don't attempt to control the reaction.

"However, if you have something like heavy water or graphite that will slow down neutrons and an absorber like cadmium, you can alter the speed of the reaction. Too much damping material will absorb too many neutrons and the reaction will stop. Not enough and the reaction will build up to an explosion. Neither of these extremes is wanted in an atomic pile. What is needed is a happy balance where you are soaking up just as many neutrons as are being generated all the time. This will give you a constant temperature inside the reactor. The net neutron reproduction constant is then 1. This balance of neutron generation and absorption is the k-factor of the reactor. Ideally 1.0000000.

"That's the ideal, though, the impossible to attain in a dynamic system like a reactor. All you need is a few more neutrons around, giving you a k-factor of 1.00000001 and you are headed for trouble. Each extra neutron produces two and your production rate soars geometrically towards bang. On the other hand, a k-factor of 0.999999999 is just as bad. Your reaction is spiraling down in the other direction. To control a pile you watch your k-factor and make constant adjustments."

"All this I follow," Costa said, "but where's the connection with Societics?"

"We'll get to that — just as soon as you realize and admit that a minute difference of degree can produce a marked difference of kind. You might say that a single, impossibly tiny, neutron is the difference between an atom bomb and a slowly cooling pile of inert uranium isotopes. Does that make sense?"

"I'm staggering, but still with you."

"Good. Then try to go along with the analogy that a human society is like an atomic pile. At one extreme you will have a dying, decadent culture — the remains of a highly mechanized society — living off its capital, using up resources it can't replace because of a lost technology. When the last machine breaks and the final food synthesizer collapses the people will die. This is the cooled down atomic pile. At the other extreme is complete and violent anarchy. Every man thinking only of himself, killing and destroying anything that gets in his way — the atomic explosion. Midway between the two is a vital, active, producing society.

"This is a generalization — and you must look at it that way. In reality society is infinitely complex, and the ramifications and possibilities are endless. It can do a lot more things than fizzle or go boom. Pressure of population, war or persecution patterns can cause waves of immigration. Plant and animal species can be wiped out by momentary needs or fashions. Remember the fate of the passenger pigeon and the American bison.

"All the pressures, cross-relationships, hungers, needs, hatreds, desires of people are reflected in their interrelationships. One man standing by himself tells us nothing. But as soon as he says something, passes on information in an altered form, or merely expresses an attitude — he becomes a reference point. He can be marked, measured and entered on a graph. His actions can be grouped with others and the action of the group measured. Man — and his society — then becomes a systems problem that can be fed into a computer. We've cut the Gordian knot of the three-L's and are on our way towards a solution."

"Stop!" Costa said, raising his hand. "I was with you as far as the 3L's. What are they? A private code?"

"Not a code — abbreviation. Linear Logic Language, the pitfall of all the old researchers. All of them, historians, sociologists, political analysts, anthropologists, were licked before they started. They had to know all about A and B before they could find C. Facts to them were always hooked up in a series. Whereas in truth they had to be analyzed as a complex circuit complete with elements like positive and negative feedback, and crossover switching. With the whole thing being stirred up constantly by continual homeostasis correction. It's little wonder they did do badly."

"You can't really say that," Adao Costa protested. "I'll admit that Societics has carried the art tremendously far ahead. But there were many basics that had already been discovered."

"If you are postulating a linear progression from the old social sciences — forget it," Neel said. "There is the same relationship here that alchemy holds to physics. The old boys with their frog guts and awful offal knew a bit about things like distilling and smelting. But there was no real order to their knowledge, and it was all an unconsidered by-product of their single goal, the whole nonsense of transmutation."

They passed a lounge, and Adao waved Neel in after him, dropping into a chair. He rummaged through his pockets for a cigarette, organizing his thoughts. "I'm still with you," he said. "But how do we work this back to the k-factor?"

"Simple," Neel told him. "Once you've gotten rid of the 3L's and their false conclusions. Remember that politics in the old days was all We are angels and They are devils. This was literally believed. In the history of mankind there has yet to be a war that wasn't backed by the official clergy on each side. And each declared that God was on their side. Which leaves You Know Who as prime supporter of the enemy. This theory is no more valid than the one that a single man can lead a country into war, followed by the inference that a well-timed assassination can save the peace."

"That doesn't sound too unreasonable," Costa said.

"Of course not. All of the old ideas sound good. They have a simple-minded simplicity that anyone can understand. That doesn't make them true. Kill a war-minded dictator and nothing changes. The violence-orientated society, the factors that produced it, the military party that represents it — none of these are changed. The k-factor remains the same."

"There's that word again. Do I get a definition yet?"

Neel smiled. "Of course. The k-factor is one of the many factors that interrelate in a society. Abstractly it is no more important than the other odd thousand we work with. But in practice it is the only one we try to alter."

"The k-factor is the war factor," Adao Costa said. All the humor was gone now.

"That's a good enough name for it," Neel said, grinding out his half-smoked cigarette. "If a society has a positive k-factor, even a slight one that stays positive, then you are going to have a war. Our planetary operators have two jobs. First to gather and interpret data. Secondly to keep the k-factor negative."

They were both on their feet now, moved by the same emotion.

"And Himmel has a positive one that stays positive," Costa said. Neel Sidorak nodded agreement. "Then let's get into the ship and get going," he said.

It was a fast trip and a faster landing. The UN cruiser cut its engines and dropped like a rock in free fall. Night rain washed the ports and the computer cut in the maximum permissible blast for the minimum time that would reduce their speed to zero at zero altitude. Deceleration sat on their chests and squeezed their bones to rubber. Something crunched heavily under their stern at the exact instant the drive cut out. Costa was unbelted and out the door while Neel was still feeling his insides shiver back into shape.

The unloading had an organized rhythm that rejected Neel. He finally realized he could help best by standing back out of the way while the crewmen grav-lifted the heavy cases out through the cargo port, into the blackness of the rain-lashed woods. Adao Costa supervised this and seemed to know what he was doing. A signal rating wearing earphones stood to one side of the lock chanting numbers that sounded like detector fixes. There was apparently enough time to unload everything — but none to spare. Things got close towards the end.

Neel was suddenly bustled out into the rain and the last two crates were literally thrown out after him. He plowed through the mud to the edge of the clearing and had just enough time to cover his face before the take-off blast burst out like a new sun.

"Sit down and relax," Costa told him. "Everything is in the green so far. The ship wasn't spotted on the way down. Now all we have to do is wait for transportation."

In theory at least, Adao Costa was Neel's assistant. In practice he took complete charge of moving their equipment and getting it under cover in the capital city of Kitezh. Men and trucks appeared to help them, and vanished as soon as their work was done. Within twenty hours they were installed in a large loft, all of the machines uncrated and plugged in. Neel took a no-sleep and began tuning checks on all the circuits, glad of something to do. Costa locked the heavy door behind their last silent helper, then dropped gratefully onto one of the bedding rolls.

"How did the gadgets hold up?" he asked.

"I'm finding out now. They're built to take punishment — but being dropped twelve feet into mud soup, then getting baked by rockets isn't in the original specs."

"They crate things well these days," Costa said unworriedly, sucking on a bottle of the famous Himmelian beer. "When do you go to work?"

"We're working right now," Neel told him, pulling a folder of papers out of the file. "Before we left I drew up a list of current magazines and newspapers I would need. You can start on these. I'll have a sampling program planned by the time you get back."

Costa groaned hollowly and reached for the papers.

*　　*　　*

Once the survey was in operation it went ahead of its own momentum. Both men grabbed what food and sleep they could. The computers gulped down Neel's figures and spat out tape-reels of answers that demanded even more facts. Costa and his unseen helpers were kept busy supplying the material.

Only one thing broke the ordered labors of the week. Neel blinked twice at Costa before his equation-fogged brain assimilated an immediate and personal factor.

"You've a bandage on your head," he said. "A *blood-stained* bandage!"

"A little trouble in the streets. Mobs. And that's an incredible feat of observation," Costa marveled. "I had the feeling that if I came in here stark naked, you wouldn't notice it."

"I . . . I get involved," Neel said. Dropping the papers on a table and kneading the tired furrow between his eyes. "Get wrapped up in the computation. Sorry. I tend to forget about people."

"Don't feel sorry to me," Costa said. "You're right. Doing the job. I'm supposed to help you, not pose for the *before* picture in Home Hospital ads. Anyway — how are we doing? Is there going to be a war? Certainly seems like one brewing outside. I've seen two people lynched who were only suspected of being Earthies."

"Looks don't mean a thing," Neel said, opening two beers. "Remember the analogy of the pile. It boils liquid metal and cooks out energy from the infrared right through to hard radiation. Yet it keeps on generating power at a nice, steady rate. But your A-bomb at zero minus one second looks as harmless as a fallen log. It's the k-factor that counts, not surface appearance. This planet may look like a dictator's dream of glory, but as long as we're reading in the negative things are fine."

"And how are things? How's our little k-factor?"

"Coming out soon," Neel said, pointing at the humming computer. "Can't tell about it yet. You never can until the computation is complete. There's a temptation to try and guess from the first figures, but they're meaningless. Like trying to predict the winner of a horse race by looking at the starters lined up at the gate."

"Lots of people think they can."

"Let them. There are few enough pleasures in this life without taking away all delusions."

Behind them the computer thunked and was suddenly still.

"This is it," Neel said, and pulled out the tape. He ran it quickly through his fingers, mumbling under his breath. Just once he stopped and set some figures into his hand computer. The result flashed in the window and he stared at it, unmoving.

"Good? Bad? What is it?"

Neel raised his head and his eyes were ten years older.

"Positive. Bad. Much worse than it was when we left Earth."

"How much time do we have?"

"Don't know for certain," Neel shrugged. "I can set it up and get an approximation. But there is no definite point on the scale where war *has* to break out. Just a going and going until, somewhere along the line —"

"I know. Gone." Costa said, reaching for his gun. He slid it into his side pocket. "Now it's time to stop looking and start doing. What do I do?"

"Going to kill War Marshal Lommeord?" Neel asked distastefully. "I thought we had settled that you can't stop a war by assassinating the top man."

"We also settled that *something* can be done to change the k-factor. The gun is for my own protection. While you're radioing results back to Earth and they're feeling bad about it, I'm going to be doing something. Now *you* tell me what that something is."

This was a different man from the relaxed and quietly efficient Adao Costa of the past week. All of his muscles were hard with the restrained energy of an animal crouching to leap. The gun, ready in his pocket, had a suddenly new significance. Neel looked away, reaching around for words. This was all very alien to him and suddenly a little frightening. It was one thing to work out a k-problem in class, and discuss the theory of correction.

It was something entirely different to direct the operation.

"Well?" Costa's voice knifed through his thoughts.

"You can . . . well . . . it's possible to change one of the peak population curves. Isolate individuals and groups, then effect status and location changes —"

"You mean get a lot of guys to take jobs in other towns through the commercial agents?"

Neel nodded.

"Too slow." Costa withered the idea with his voice. "Fine in the long run, but of absolutely no value in an emergency." He began to pace back and forth. Too quickly. It was more of a bubbling-over than a relaxation. "Can't you isolate some recent key events that can be reversed?"

"It's possible." Neel thought about it, quickly. "It wouldn't be a final answer, just a delaying action."

"That's good enough. Tell me what to do."

Neel flipped through his books of notes, checking off the Beta-13's. These were the reinforcers, the individuals and groups who were k-factor amplifiers. It was a long list which he cut down quickly by crossing off the low increment additions and multiple groups. Even while the list was incomplete, Neel began to notice a pattern. It was an unlikely one, but it was there. He isolated the motivator and did a frequency check. Then sat back and whistled softly.

"We have a powerhouse here," he said, flipping the paper across the table. "Take this organization out of the equations and you might even knock us negative."

"Society for the Protection of the Native Born," Costa read. "Doesn't sound like very important. Who or what are they?"

"Proof positive of the law of averages. It's possible to be dealt a royal flush in a hand of cards, but it isn't very common. It's just as possible for a bunch of simpletons to set up an organization for one purpose, and have it turn out to be a supercharged, high-frequency k-factor amplifier. That's what's happened with this infernal S.P.N.B. A seedy little social club, dedicated to jingoists with low I.Q.'s. With the war scare they have managed to get hold of a few credits. They have probably been telling the same inflated stories for years about the discrimination against natives of this fair planet, but no one has really cared. Now they have a chance to get their news releases and faked pix out in quantity. Just at a time when the public is ripe for their brand of nonsense. Putting this bunch out of business will be a good day's work."

"Won't there be repercussions?" Costa asked. "If they are this important and throw so much weight around — won't it look suspicious if they are suddenly shut up. Like an obvious move by the enemy?"

"Not at all. That might be true if, for instance, you blew up the headquarters of the War Party. It would certainly be taken as an aggressive move. But no one really knows or cares about this Society of the Half-baked Native Born. There might be reaction and interest if attention was drawn to them. But if some accident or act of nature were to put them out of business, that would be the end of it."

Costa was snapping his lighter on and off as he listened to Neel, staring at the flame. He closed it and held it up. "I believe in accidents. I believe that even in our fireproof age, fires still occur. Buildings still burn down. And if a burnt building just happened to be occupied by the S.P.N.B. — just one tenant of many — and their offices and records were destroyed; that would be of very little interest to anyone except the fire brigade."

"You're a born criminal," Neel told him. "I'm glad we're on the same side. That's your department and I leave it to you. I'll just listen for the news flashes. Meanwhile I have one little errand to take care of."

The words stopped Costa, who was almost out the door. He turned stiffly to look at Neel putting papers into an envelope. Yet Costa spoke naturally, letting none of his feelings through into his voice.

"Where are you going?"

"To see Hengly, the planetary operator here. Abravanel told me to stay away from him, to run an entirely new basic survey. Well we've done that now, and pinpointed some of the trouble areas as well. I can stop feeling guilty about poaching another man's territory and let him know what's going on."

"No. Stay away from Hengly," Costa said. "The last thing in the world we want to do, is to be seen near him. There's a chance that he . . . well . . . might be compromised."

"What do you mean!" Neel snapped. "Hengly's a friend of mine, a graduate —"

"He might also be surrounded ten deep by the secret police. Did you stop to think about *that*?"

Neel hadn't thought about it, and his anger vanished when he did. Costa drove the point home.

"Societics has been a well kept secret for over two centuries. It may still be a secret — or bits of it might have leaked out. And even if the Himmelians know nothing about Societics, they have certainly heard of espionage. They know the UN has agents on their world, they might think Hengly is one of them. This is all speculation, of course, but we do have one fact — this Society of Native Boobs we turned up. *We* had no trouble finding them. If Hengly had reliable field men, he should know about them, too. The only reason he hasn't is because he isn't getting the information. Which means he's compromised."

Reaching back for a chair, Neel fell heavily into it. "You're right . . . of course! I never realized."

"Good," Costa said. "We'll do something to help Hengly tomorrow, but this operation comes first. Sit tight. Get some rest. And don't open the door for anyone except me."

It had been a long job — and a tiring one — but it was almost over. Neel allowed himself the luxury of a long yawn, then shuffled over to the case of rations they had brought. He stripped the seal from something optimistically labeled CHICKEN DINNER — it tasted just like the algae it had been made from — and boiled some coffee while it was heating.

And all the time he was doing these prosaic tasks his mind was turning an indigestible fact over and over. It wasn't a conscious process, but it was nevertheless going on. The automatic mechanism of his brain ran it back and forth like a half heard tune, searching for its name. Neel was tired, or he would have reacted sooner. The idea finally penetrated. One fact he had taken for granted was an obvious impossibility.

The coffee splashed to the floor as he jumped to his feet.

"It's wrong . . . it *has* to be wrong!" he said aloud, grabbing up the papers. Computations and graphs dropped and were trampled into the spilled coffee. When he finally found the one he wanted his hands were shaking as he flipped through it. The synopsis of Hengly's reports for the past five years. The gradual rise and fall of the k-factor from month to month. There were no sharp breaks in the curve or gaps in the supporting equations.

Societics isn't an exact science. But it's exact enough to know when it is working with incomplete or false information. If Hengly had been kept in the dark about the S.P.N.B., he would also have been misinformed about other factors. This kind of alteration of survey would *have* to show in the equations.

It didn't.

Time was running out and Neel had to act. But what to do? He must warn Adao Costa. And the records here had to be protected. Or better yet destroyed. There was a power in these machines and charts that couldn't be allowed to fall into nationalist hands. But what could be done about it?

In all the welter of equipment and containers, there was one solid, heavy box that he had never opened. It belonged to Costa, and the UN man had never unlocked it in his presence. Neel looked at the heavy clasps on it and felt defeat. But when he pulled at the lid, wondering what to do next, it fell open. It hadn't been sealed. Costa wasn't the kind of man who did things by accident. He had looked forward to the time when Neel might need what was in this box, and had it ready.

Inside was just what Neel expected. Grenades, guns, some smoothly polished devices that held an aura of violence. Looking at them, Neel had an overwhelming sensation of defeat. His life was dedicated to peace and the furthering of peace. He hated the violence that seemed inborn in man, and detested all the hypocritical rationalizations, such as the ends justifying the means. All of his training and personal inclinations were against it.

And he reached down and removed the blunt, black gun.

There was one other thing he recognized in the compact arsenal — a time bomb. There had been lectures on this mechanism in school, since the fact was clearly recognized that a time might come when equipment had to be destroyed rather than fall into the wrong hands. He had never seen one since, but he had learned the lesson well. Neel pushed the open chest nearer to his instruments and set the bomb dial for fifteen minutes. He slipped the gun into his pocket, started the fuse, and carefully locked the door when he left.

The bridges were burned. Now he had to find Adao Costa.

This entire operation was outside of his experience and knowledge. He could think of no plan that could possibly make things easier or safer. All he could do was head for the offices of the Society for the Protection of the Native Born and hope he could catch Adao before he ran into any trouble.

Two blocks away from the address he heard the sirens. Trying to act as natural as the other pedestrians, he turned to look as the armored cars and trucks hurtled by. Packed with armed police, their sirens and revolving lights cleared a path through the dark streets. Neel kept walking, following the cars now.

The street he wanted to go into was cordoned off.

Showing more than a normal interest would have been a giveaway. He let himself be hurried past, with no more than a glance down the block, with the other pedestrians. Cars and men were clustered around a doorway that Neel felt sure was number 265, his destination. Something was very wrong.

Had Costa walked into a trap — or tripped an alarm? It didn't really matter which, either way the balloon had gone up. Neel walked on slowly, painfully aware of his own inadequacy in dealing with the situation. It was a time for action — but what action? He hadn't the slightest idea where Costa was or how he could be of help to him.

Halfway down the block there was a dark mouth of an alleyway — unguarded. Without stopping to think, Neel turned into it. It would bring him closer to the building. Perhaps Costa was still trapped in there. He could get in, help him.

The back of 265 was quiet, with no hint of the activity on the other side of the building. Neel had counted carefully and was sure he had the right one. It was completely dark in the unlit alley, but he found a recessed door by touch. The chances were it was locked, but he moved into the alcove and leaned his weight against it, pulling at the handle, just in case. Nothing moved.

An inch behind his back the alley filled with light, washed with it, eye burning and strong. His eyes snapped shut, but he forced them open again, blinking against the pain. There were searchlights at each end of the alley, sealing it off. He couldn't get out.

In the instant before the fear hit him he saw the blood spots on the ground. There were three of them, large and glistening redly wet. They extended in a straight line away from him, pointing towards the gaping entrance of a cellar.

When the lights went out, Neel dived headlong towards the cracked and filthy pavement. The darkness meant that the police were moving slowly towards him from both ends of the alley, trapping him in between. There was nothing doubtful about the fate of an armed Earthman caught here. He didn't care. Neel's fear wasn't gone — he just had not time to think about it. His long shot had paid off and there was still a chance he could get Costa out of the trap he had let him walk into.

The lights had burned an after-image into his retina. Before it faded he reached out and felt his fingers slide across the dusty ground into a patch of wetness. He scrubbed at it with his sleeve, soaking up the blood, wiping the spot fiercely. With his other hand he pushed together a pile of dust and dirt, spreading it over the stain. As soon as he was sure the stain was covered he slid forward, groping for the second telltale splash.

Time was his enemy and he had no way to measure it. He could have been lying in the rubble of that alley for an hour — or a second. What was to be done, had to be done at once without a sound. There were silent, deadly men coming towards him through the darkness.

After the second smear was covered there was a drawn out moment of fear when he couldn't find the third and last. His fingers touched it finally, much farther on than he had expected. Time had certainly run out. Yet he forced himself to do as good a job here as he had with the other two. Only when it was dried and covered did he allow himself to slide forward into the cellar entrance.

Everything was going too fast. He had time for a single deep breath before the shriek of a whistle paralyzed him again. Footsteps slapped towards him and one of the searchlights burned with light. The footsteps speeded up and the man ran by, close enough for Neel to touch if he had reached out a hand. His clothing was shapeless and torn, his head and face thick with hair. That was all

Neel had time to see before the guns roared and burned the life from the runner.

Some derelict, sleeping in the alley, who had paid with his life for being in the wrong spot at the wrong time. But his death had bought Neel a little more time. He turned and looked into the barrel of a gun.

Shock after shock had destroyed his capacity for fear. There was nothing left that could move him, even his own death. He looked quietly — dully — at the muzzle of the gun. With slow determination his mind turned over and he finally realized that this time there was nothing to fear.

"It's me, Adao," he whispered. "You'll be all right now."

"Ahh, it is you —" the voice came softly out of the darkness, the gun barrel wavered and sank. "Lift me up so I can get at this door. Can't seem to stand too well any more."

Neel reached down, found Costa's shoulders and slowly dragged him to his feet. His eyes were adjusting to the glare above them now, and he could make out the gleam of reflected light on the metal in Costa's fingers. The UN man's other hand was clutched tightly to his waist. The gun had vanished. The metal device wasn't a key, but Costa used it like one. It turned in the lock and the door swung open under their weight. Neel half carried, half dragged the other man's dead weight through it, dropping him to the floor inside. Before he closed the door he reached down and felt a great pool of blood outside.

There was no time to do a perfect job, the hard footsteps were coming, just a few yards away. His sleeves were sodden with blood as he blotted, then pushed rubble into the stain. He pulled back inside and the door closed with only the slightest click.

"I don't know how you managed it, but I'm glad you found me," Costa said. There was weakness as well as silence in his whisper.

"It was only chance I found you," Neel said bitterly. "But criminal stupidity on my part that let you walk into this trap."

"Don't worry about it, I knew what I was getting into. But I still had to go. Spring the trap to see if it *was* a trap."

"You suspected then that Hengly was —" Neel couldn't finish the sentence. He knew what he wanted to say, but the idea was too unbearable to put into words. Costa had no such compunction.

"Yes. Dear Hengly, graduate of the University and Practitioner of Societics. A traitor. A warmonger, worse than any of his predecessors because he knew just what to sell and how to sell it. It's never happened before . . . but there was always the chance . . . the weight of responsibility was too much . . . he gave in —" Costa's voice had died away almost to a whisper. Then it was suddenly loud again, no louder than normal speaking volume, but sounding like a shout in the secret basement.

"Neel!"

"It's all right. Take it easy —"

"Nothing is all right — don't you realize that. I've been sending my reports back, so the UN and your Societics people will know how to straighten this mess out. But Hengly can turn this world upside down and might even get a shooting-war going before they get here. I'm out of it, but I can tell you who to contact, people who'll help. Hold the k-factor down —"

"That wouldn't do any good," Neel said quietly. "The whole thing is past the patch and polish stage now. Besides — I blew the whole works up. My machines and records, your —"

"You're a fool!" For the first time there was pain in Costa's voice.

"No. I was before — but not any more. As long as I thought it was a normal problem I was being outguessed at every turn. You must understand the ramifications of Societics. To a good operator there is no interrelationship that cannot be uncovered. Hengly would be certain to keep his eyes open for another field check. Our kind of operation is very easy to spot if you know where — and how — to look. The act of getting information implies contact of some kind, that contact can be detected. He's had our location marked and has been sitting tight, buying time. But our time ran out when you showed them we were ready to fight back. That's why I destroyed our setup, and cut our trail."

"But . . . then we're defenseless! What can we possibly do?"

Neel knew the answer, but he hesitated to put it into words. It would be final then. He suddenly realized he had forgotten about Costa's wound.

"I'm sorry . . . I forgot about your being hurt. What can I do?"

"Nothing," Costa snapped. "I put a field dressing on, that'll do. Answer my question. What is there left? What can be done now?"

"I'll have to kill Hengly. That will set things right until the team gets here."

"But what good will that accomplish?" Costa asked, trying to see the other man in the darkness of the cellar. "You told me yourself that a war couldn't be averted by assassination. No one individual means that much."

"Only in a normal situation," Neel explained. "You must look at the power struggle between planets as a kind of celestial chess game. It has its own rules. When I talked about individuals earlier I was talking about pieces on this chessboard. What I'm proposing now is a little more dramatic. I'm going to win the chess game in a slightly more unorthodox way. I'm going to shoot the other chess player."

There was silence for a long moment, broken only by the soft sigh of their breathing. Then Costa stirred and there was the sound of metal clinking slightly on the floor.

"It's really my job," Costa said, "but I'm no good for it. You're right, you'll have to go. But I can help you, plan it so you will be able to get to Hengly. You might even stand a better chance than me, because you are so obviously an amateur. Now listen carefully, because we haven't much time."

Neel didn't argue. He knew what needed doing, but Costa could tell him how best to go about it. The instructions were easy to memorize, and he put the weapons away as he was told.

"Once you're clear of this building, you'll have to get cleaned up," Costa said. "But that's the only thing you should stop for. Get to Hengly while he is still rattled, catch him off guard as much as possible. Then — after you finish with him — dig yourself in. Stay hidden at least three days before you try to make any contacts. Things should have quieted down a bit by then."

"I don't like leaving you here," Neel said.

"It's the best way, as well as being the only way. I'll be safe enough. I've a nice little puncture in me, but there's enough medication to see me through."

"If I'm going to hole up, I'll hole up here. I'll be back to take care of you."

Costa didn't answer him. There was nothing more to say. They shook hands in the darkness and Neel crawled away.

There was little difficulty in finding the front door of the building, but Neel hesitated before he opened it. Costa had been sure Neel could get away without being noticed, but he didn't feel so sure himself. There certainly would be plenty of police in the streets, even here. Only as he eased the door did he understand why Costa had been so positive about this.

Gunfire hammered somewhere behind him; other guns answered. Costa must have had another gun. He had planned it this way and the best thing Neel could do was not to think about it and go ahead with the plan. A car whined by in the roadway. As soon as it had passed Neel slipped out and crossed the empty street to the nearest monosub entrance. Most of the stations had valet machines.

It was less than an hour later when he reached Hengly's apartment. Washed, shaved — and with his clothes cleaned — Neel felt a little more sure of himself. No one had stopped him or even noticed him. The lobby had been empty and the automatic elevator left him off at the right floor when he gave it Hengly's name. Now, facing the featureless door, he had a sharp knife of fear. It was too easy. He reached out slowly and tried the handle. The door was unlocked. Taking a deep breath, he opened it and stepped inside.

It was a large room, but unlit. An open door at the other end had a dim light shining through it. Neel started that way and pain burst in his head, spinning him down, face forward.

He never quite lost consciousness, but details were vague in his memory. When full awareness returned he realized that the lights were on in the room. He was lying on his back, looking up at them. Two men stood next to him, staring down at him from above the perspective columns of their legs. One held a short metal bar that he kept slapping into his open palm.

The other man was Hengly.

"Not very friendly for an old classmate," he said, holding out

Neel's gun. "Now get inside, I want to talk to you."

Neel rolled over painfully and crawled to his feet. His head throbbed with pain, but he tried to ignore it. As he stood up his hand brushed his ankle. The tiny gun Costa had given him was still in the top of his shoe. Perhaps Hengly wasn't being as smart as he should.

"I can take care of him," Hengly said to the man with the metal rod. "He's the only one left now, so you can get some sleep. See you early in the morning though." The man nodded agreement and left.

Slouched in the chair Neel looked forward to a certain pleasure in killing Hengly. Costa was dead, and this man was responsible for his death. It wouldn't even be like killing a friend, Hengly was very different from the man he had known. He had put on a lot of weight and affected a thick beard and flowing mustache. There was something jovial and paternal about him — until you looked into his eyes. Neel slumped forward, worn out, letting his fingers fall naturally next to the gun in his shoe. Hengly couldn't see his hand, the desk was in the way. All Neel had to do was draw and fire.

"You can pull out the gun," Hengly said with a grim smile, "but don't try to shoot it." He had his own gun now, aimed directly at Neel. Leaning forward he watched as Neel carefully pulled out the tiny weapon and threw it across the room. "That's better," he said, placing his own gun on the desk where he could reach it easily. "Now we can talk."

"There's nothing I have to say to you, Hengly." Neel leaned back in the chair, exhausted. "You're a traitor!"

Hengly hammered the desk in sudden anger and shouted. "Don't talk to me of treachery, my little man of peace. Creeping up with a gun to kill a friend. Is that peaceful? Where are the ethos of humanism now, you were very fond of them when we were in the University!"

Neel didn't want to listen to the words, he thought instead of how right Costa had been. He was dead, but this was still his operation. It was going according to plan.

"Walk right in there," Costa had said. "He won't kill you. Not at first, at least. He's the loneliest man in the universe, because he has given up one world for another that he hasn't gained yet. There will be no one he can confide in. He'll know you have come to kill him, but he won't be able to resist talking to you first. Particularly if you make it easy for him to defeat you. Not too easy — he must feel he is outthinking you. You'll have a gun for him to take away, but that will be too obvious. This small gun will be hidden as well, and when he finds that, too, he should be taken off his guard. Not much, but enough for you to kill him. Don't wait. Do it at the first opportunity."

Out of the corner of his eye, Neel could see the radiophone clipped to the front of his jacket. It was slightly tarnished, looking like any one of ten thousand in daily use — almost a duplicate of the one Hengly wore. A universal symbol of the age, like the keys and small change in his pockets.

Only Neel's phone was a deadly weapon. Product of a research into sudden death that he had never been aware of before. All he had to do was get it near Hengly, the mechanism had been armed when he put it on. It had a range of two feet. As soon as it was that far from any part of his body it would be actuated.

"Can I ask you a question, Hengly?" His words cut loudly through the run of the other man's speech.

Hengly frowned at the interruption, then nodded permission. "Go ahead," he said. "What would you like to know?"

"The obvious. Why did you do it? Change sides I mean. Give up a positive work, for this . . . this negative corruption. . . ."

"That's how much you know about it." Hengly was shouting now. "Positive, negative. War, peace. Those are just words, and it took me years to find it out. What could be more positive than making something of my life — and of this planet at the same time. It's in my power to do it, and I've done it."

"Power, perhaps that's the key word," Neel said, suddenly very tired. "We have the stars now but we have carried with us our little personal lusts and emotions. There's nothing wrong with that, I suppose, as long as we keep them personal. It's when we start inflicting them on others the trouble starts. Well, it's over now. At least this time."

With a single, easy motion he unclipped the radiophone and flipped it across the desk towards Hengly.

"Good-by," he said.

The tiny mechanism clattered onto the desk and Hengly leaped back, shouting hoarsely. He pulled the gun up and tried to aim at the radiophone and at Neel at the same time. It was too late to do either. There was a brief humming noise from the phone.

Neel jerked in his chair. It felt as if a slight electric shock had passed through him. He had felt only a microscopic percentage of the radiation.

Hengly got it all. The actuated field of the device had scanned his nervous system, measured and tested it precisely. Then adjusted itself to the exact micro-frequency that carried the messages in his efferent nervous system. Once the adjustment had been made, the charged condensers had released their full blasts of energy on that frequency.

The results were horribly dramatic. Every efferent neuron in his system carried the message full power. Every muscle in his body responded with a contraction of full intensity.

Neel closed his eyes, covered them, turned away gasping. It couldn't be watched. An epileptic in a seizure can break the bones in a leg or arm by simultaneous contraction of opposing muscles. When all the opposed muscles of Hengly's body did this the results were horrible beyond imagining.

When Neel recovered a measure of sanity he was in the street, running. He slowed to a walk, and looked around. It was just dawn and the streets were empty. Ahead was the glowing entrance of a monotube and he headed for it. The danger was over now, as long as he was careful.

Pausing on the top step, he breathed the fresh air of the new morning. There was a sighing below as an early train pulled into the station. The dawn-lit sky was the color of blood.

"Blood," he said aloud. Then, "Do we have to keep on killing? Isn't there another way?"

He started guiltily as his voice echoed in the empty street, but no one had heard him.

Quickly, two at a time, he ran down the steps.

Lightning Source UK Ltd.
Milton Keynes UK
UKHW010648190720
366759UK00001B/67